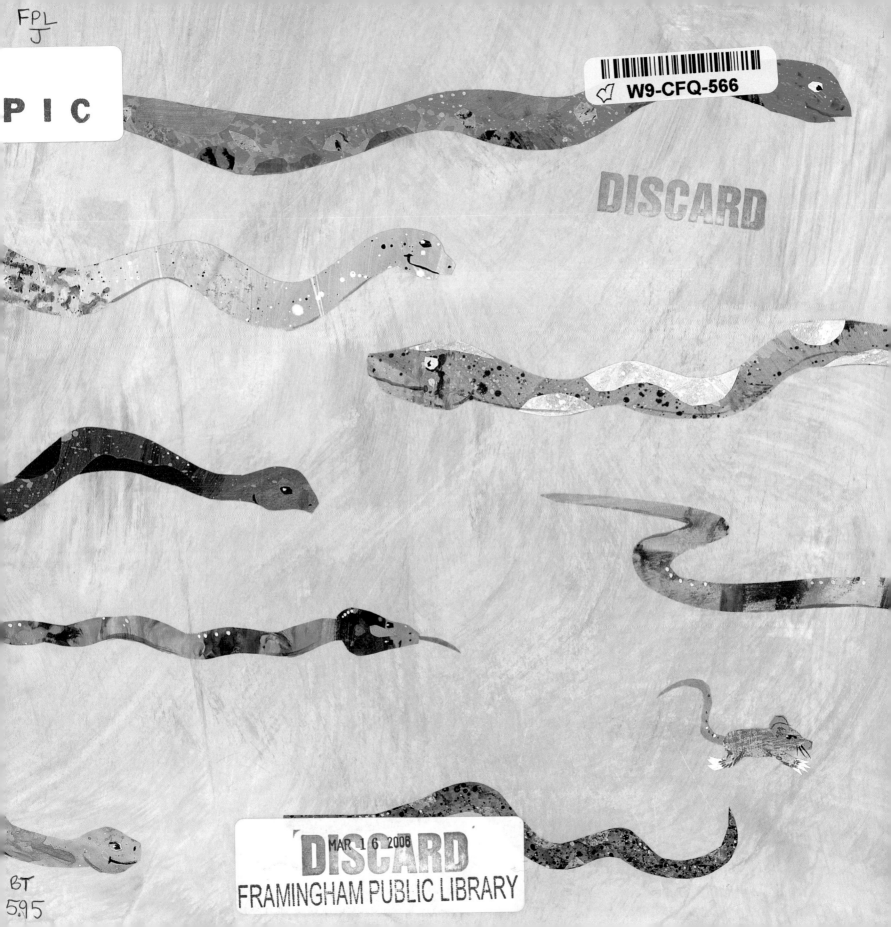

To future herpetologists – A.W.

For Scott Wadler, Jaimie Karas
and Lisa McCourt – C.N.

Published in the United States of America by Star Bright Books, Inc., New York.
The name Star Bright Books and the Star Bright Books logo are registered
trademarks of Star Bright Books, Inc. Please visit www.starbrightbooks.com.

ISBN 1-932065-96-2

Printed in China 9 8 7 6 5 4 3 2 1

Library of Congress Cataloging-in-Publication Data

Weston, Anne, 1956-
  My brother needs a boa / by Anne Weston ; illustrated by Cheryl Nathan.
     p. cm.
  Summary: When a rat moves into Benito's rainforest village store and chases away all the
customers, he tries to find the perfect boa constrictor to get rid of the rat.
    ISBN 1-932065-96-2
  [1. Boa constrictor--Fiction. 2. Snakes--Fiction. 3. Rain forests--Fiction. 4. Stores, Retail--Fiction.]
  I. Nathan, Cheryl, 1958- ill. II. Title.

PZ7.W5262825Myab 2005
[E]--dc22
                                        2004029604

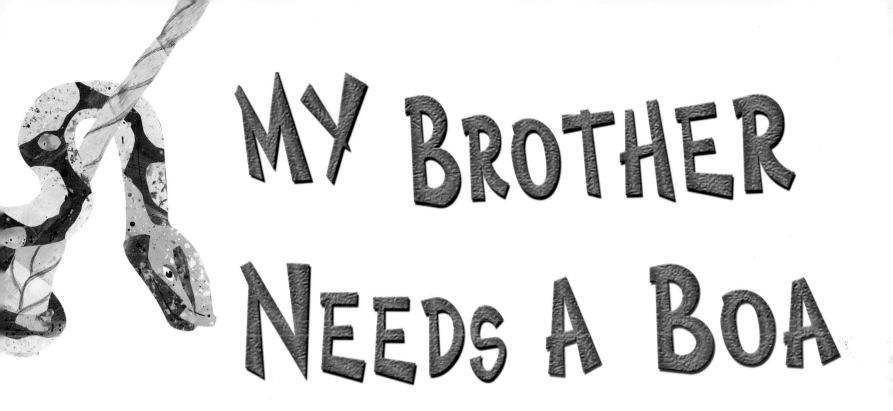

My Brother Needs A Boa

By Anne Weston
Illustrations by Cheryl Nathan

Star Bright Books
New York

Benito lives in a rainforest. Monkeys, anteaters, ocelots, and boas live in the rainforest too. Benito's house is in a village beside a river.

Coconut palms line the streets of Benito's village. Every house has flowers in its yard. The roofs of the houses are made of palm leaves.

Benito likes the soft sound the rain makes falling on the palm-leaf roof. He likes to rest in his hammock at the end of the day and listen to the rain.

Benito has built a little store onto one side of his house. Before Benito built his store, when people in the village needed flour to bake bread, or medicine for a sick cow, or rope to make a horse bridle, they had to paddle their boats a long way down the river to the store in the next village. They had to start when the sun rose, and they didn't get back until the sun set.

Benito's neighbors arc happy to have a store in their own village now. Benito is happy too. He likes to talk to his neighbors when they come into the store to shop.

But last week calamity struck.

On Sunday a strong wind blew through the village.
It rattled the palm leaves on the roofs of the houses:
It tore the petals off the flowers in the yards.
It blew a monkey right out of a mango tree
and shook the palm trees so hard coconuts
rained down on the village street.

On Monday morning Mrs. Murillo came into Benito's store. "The wind blew down four coconuts in front of my house," she said. "I need brown sugar to make coconut candy."

Benito showed her the brown sugar on the shelf. Each chunk of sugar was carefully wrapped in corn shucks to keep it clean.

Mrs. Murillo picked up a chunk of sugar. She looked at the corn shuck wrapper.

"EEK!" she shrieked. "A RAT has gnawed this sugar. There's a hole in the wrapper and I see the rat's teeth-marks." She dropped the sugar and ran out of the store.

Mrs. Murillo yelled to her husband, "Olimpo, get our boat ready! You must paddle me to the store in the next village. There's a RAT in Benito's store!"

Everyone in the village heard Mrs. Murillo. "Benito has a rat in his store!" they said. "We like Benito, but we don't want to shop in a store with a rat."

Monday afternoon no one came to Benito's store.

Benito searched for the rat. He looked behind the candles that people bought to light their houses. He checked under the pieces of cardboard that held fish-hooks for fishing in the river. He peeked inside the rubber boots that people wore in the mud. He lifted the sacks of corn that people bought to feed their chickens. But he could not find the rat.

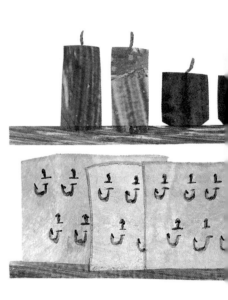

At last Benito saw the rat's whiskers sticking out from behind the umbrellas! He grabbed a broom and swished it down. But quick as a snap, the rat vanished.

"I'll never get that rat out of here," Benito told his sister Vilma when she came to visit. "People will never come back to my store. What can I do?"

"You need a boa," Vilma told him. "The boa will chase the rat out of the store."

"What a good idea!" Benito said. "But how will I get a boa?"

"Don't worry," Vilma said. "I'll help you."

Tuesday morning Vilma walked to the river to wash clothes.
"My brother needs a boa," she told the other ladies as they
scrubbed their laundry spotless on the rocks at the edge of the river.

The other ladies nodded. "We heard about the rat," they said.

Tuesday afternoon Vilma rode her pony to her cousin
Estela's house to help Estela make water-apple jelly.
"My brother needs a boa," Vilma told her.
Soon everyone in the village knew Benito needed a boa.

Wednesday morning Benito heard horse hooves clip-clopping up to the store. "Benito!" called his neighbor Julio, "I brought you a boa." Julio tied his horse to a mango tree and walked into the store. A small snake was wound around his arm.

"That boa is too small!" Benito said. "*Gracias*, but I want a boa that's big enough to start work today. Turn it loose in the rainforest."

Wednesday afternoon Benito heard the squeaking of ox-cart wheels outside the store.

"Benito!" called Benito's neighbor Rafael. "I've brought you a boa. Come and see."

Benito went outside. He looked in the ox-cart. A snake thicker than his leg lay zigzagged across the bottom of the cart.

"That boa is twice as long as I am," Benito said. "It's too big. If Mrs. Murillo grabs it by accident when she reaches for the clothespins, she'll scream and ruin my business again. *Gracias*, but I want a boa that won't take up a whole shelf of my store by itself. Turn it loose in the rainforest."

Thursday morning Estela's daughter Estelita skipped into the store. Over her shoulder she carried a bag she had woven from string. She had made the string from tree bark.

"Benito, I brought you a boa," she said.

Benito looked in the bag. A long piece of vine was twisted up in the bag. Then Benito realized the vine was really a thin brown snake.

"That's not a boa," he said. "That's a vine snake. It won't scare the rat. *Gracias*, but I want a boa. Turn it loose in the rainforest."

Thursday afternoon
Mr. Murillo came to
the store. "Benito, I
brought you a boa," he
said. "It's in my boat at
the edge of the river."

Benito walked to the river with
Mr. Murillo. He looked in the boat.

A boa lay stretched out beside the
anchor rope. The boa wasn't too big
and it wasn't too small, but it looked fat.

"That boa just ate," Benito said. "It won't
want to move for a week. *Gracias*, but I want
a boa that is ready to chase the rat away now.
Turn it loose in the rainforest."

Benito walked sadly back to his store.
No one was there to buy anything.

Night was coming. Benito climbed into his
hammock and worried. "What will I do if
no one ever comes to my store again?" he thought.

Then a long, low shadow slipped through the open doorway.
Without a sound, the shadow slithered across the floor.
It crept up the wall to Benito's hammock rope.

Benito felt his hammock tremble. The rope began to move.

Benito leaned forward. A brown and black and yellow snake,
not too small, not too big, not too thin, and not too fat,
twined around his hammock rope.

The boa looked at Benito. Benito looked at the boa.
Then the boa skimmed up the rope and
disappeared in the darkness where the
wall met the palm-leaf roof.

Friday morning Benito was sweeping the store when he glimpsed a flash of movement in the corner near the umbrellas. A furry gray bundle scurried out and dashed toward the open door. Behind it flowed the boa like a thick stream of chocolate syrup.

The tip of the rat's tail disappeared through the doorway. The boa turned and glided back to the umbrellas. "*Gracias*," Benito said to the boa.

"The rat is gone," Benito told his sister Vilma when she came into the store at lunchtime.

Friday afternoon Vilma picked yellow star fruit from a tree in her yard. She took the star fruit to Mr. and Mrs. Murillo's house. "My brother has a boa now," she told them. "The rat is gone."

"Good!" said Mrs. Murillo.
"I need matches to light my cookstove.
I'll buy them at Benito's store."

Saturday morning Vilma milked her cow and made cheese. She wrapped a ball of cheese in a banana leaf and took it to her cousin Estela's house.

"My brother has a boa now," she said. "The rat is gone."

"Good!" said Estela. "I need corn to feed my chickens. I'll send Estelita to get some from Benito's store."

Saturday afternoon Vilma went to the river to wash clothes.
"My brother has a boa now," she told the other ladies.
"The rat is gone."

"Good!" they said. "Whose boa did he choose?"

Vilma laughed. "He didn't choose anyone's boa," she said.
"The boa chose Benito!"